INTERLOPERS

A FORBIDDEN WORLD

BUHLER

Interlopers: A Forbidden World

Copyright © 2025 Buhler

ISBN (Paperback): 978-1-965687-94-9
ISBN (eBook): 978-1-965687-95-6

All rights reserved. No part of this book may be used or reproduced by any means, graphic, electronic, or mechanical, including photocopying, recording, taping or by information storage and retrieval system without the written permission of the author except in the case of brief quotations embodied in critical articles and reviews.

Because of the dynamic nature of the Internet, any web addresses or links contained in this book may have changed since publication and may no longer be valid. The views expressed in the work are solely those of the author and do not necessarily reflect the views of the publisher, and the publisher hereby disclaims any responsibility for them.

Printed in the United States of America.

Auctorem House
276 5th Ave, Ste 704-2591
New York, NY 10001
www.auctoremhouse.com
1.888.332.7718

CONTENTS

OUR STORY BEGINS

A frightening Amazon Jungle river tale about three sets of interlopers Through their own greed and need of self importance in holding the world and the entire solar system in jeopardy, and danger by confronting "The RAL", are alien interlopers who came to the Amazon jungle rainforest, and once there decided not to leave this ice-blue world we call "Earth".

CAST OF CHARACTERS

Nicole Hanes

Hugo Hartford

Jonathan Weissk

Jennifer (Waitress)

Mr. Greenwaldl

Charles Evers

Paula Evers

Mr. Terrance Smyth

Mr. Clive Bangor

Dr. Neville Pennyworth

Mr. Wesley Ross Pickford

Detective Torres

Mr. Clive Ackserson

Emmanuelle Ramon

Sabastian (Porter)

Captain (Porter)

Samuel (Porter)

Mr. Michael Renner

Fran Weiss

Isabel Torres

Benjamin Stokes[0]

Dr. Aldor Bormann

Colonel Eduardo Harras

EPISODE

IN THE BEGINNING

AN AMAZON'S JOURNEY

IN 2016, AN alone naturalist (Jonathan Weiss) on his reconditioned armored outfitted river houseboat called "What's Next" is leaning against a second floor deck railings and looks out and down unto the beautiful majestic Amazon basin jungle river slowly going by at five knots enjoying a half lighted lucky strike menthol cigarette, and sipping on his flask filled with jack daniels bourbon alcohol drink and wondering what it would take and professionally mean for him to capture this all powerful beast that he now stalks.

He takes out from his pocket his news clippings from two years ago showing the brutal and savage killings of the tribal indian couple resting by this great waterfall lake that I am headed too, and leaving behind a nine inch incisor tooth he is carrying in his satchel bag he got paid for from the brazilian police detective for this region, Det. Raphael Torres and his small police department forensic lab unit, in not knowing how this came about, or who would do such horrible homicidal act on two young people in their early twenties in our amazon community.

While resting on the boat's railings sipping his jack daniels bourbon and watching the piranhas below looking for food and viciously attacking its prey, if it finds them Mr. Weiss, then looking out into the jungle had a memory flashback in London almost two months ago…

A BRITANNIA MEETING FOR ALL

WHILE IN LONDON at the Royal Safari Club, at the Royal Carlyle Hotel and conference Center near Trafalgar Square. While there he attended the Anglo-American Adventurers Club and the annual international get together of scientists, archaeologist, Museum Directors and Curators, and the very rich people who support and donate them so hard in which they work so hard with others in politics in preventing and stopping wars and religious geopolitical discourse, and also the weathering and erosion from nature in the imperiling and destruction of our lost ancient temples, statues and ruins and in the what may become of them in the future.

knowledge of who we are as mankind and our limited and brief understanding of who and where we came from in our ancient lineage of humanity, before five thousand years of pre (B.C.E.) history.

Each and every guest and influential speaker was telling their own personal life's story about themselves and what they are doing now, and what they are doing to preserve and save our humanities historical past all over the world. The so-called who's who in the field of archeology, antiquities, government and private companies and how they are keeping the history of man alive and how we managed and evolved with our natural surroundings that were primitive by becoming more successful and cultural driven (tribes, nations) in providing a better more peaceful as opposed to war for each generation to come.

INTERNATIONAL CLUBBING

WHILE MR. JONATHAN Weiss, was attending the royal Carlyle hotel and the Anglo-American club and international conference, Mr. Weiss, decided to go to the international adventurers club, 'British Empire Colonial

Tavern', walking inside the main salon of the hotel next to the main very large lobby of the saloon that contains on one side a prehistoric petrified wooden statue and a marble stone three foot high pedital of a changing bull elephant from rhodesia, circa, 1921. And on the other side a maned male roaring lion also from rhodesia about six feet long and tail, ready to strike and pounce, and kill an antelope from a specially designed rocks that is eight foot high in a glass enclosed around a marble stone three foot high located on the other walk inside of the main lobby next to the 'British Empire Tavern.'

HOW ABOUT SOME FOOD AND DRINK

British Club Hotel

AND, FROM HE'S watching the lion and looking around this fascinating lobby, Mr. Jonathan Weiss, then walks through the twin twelve foot high wooden oak and crystal glass doors into the British Empire Tavern And walking by two wax figures of Queen Victoria and Sir Sir Winston Churchill, and going to t hostess greeting podium and a waiting server who then greets greets and escorts him to one of the wickers tables near the seven walled seventy inch (TV) tube screens. Then he sits down on a wicker and leather seated chair under a soft rotating six foot fan blade, and now sitting down into this three semi-round wicker and marble stone table and into this very comfortable leather cushion seated chair and is now ready to order an american colossal shrimp cocktail with a 22-ounce crystal house glass of Newcastle ale beer, sitting in a cool air-conditioned bar, sitting under a wicker leather chair under a whirling spinning fan looking at the BBC news with its bulletins and headline news. Then a cute, very attractive English blonde bar maiden (waitress) comes along (named Jennifer) and says to him what are you having in looking at his conference lapel badge name? To Mr Weiss, here today, and he said to her, that I am ordering a colossal shrimp cocktail with a 22-ounce cold glass of Newcastle ale beer to her, she left and two minutes later she came back with his shrimp and cold tap ale beer and thanking her, that she was so prompt as could be, and again thanking her for being a good server with a five pound note tip. Then before she leaves he ask her what is behind and top off tha long perhaps eighty foot bar, and she said back to me, you are quit correct about the length of the bar, and then she said that there are two very large, one hundred and twenty-one inch plasma monitor (TV) screens separated by five analogue atomic timing clocks with the center one controlling every fifteen minutes different scenes around the world, under the sea and into outer space. Right now you are watching on the left screen the temple ruins in south eastern Myanmar, and on the right monitor screen you are looking at the western Amazon river basin, showing sixty piranha fish enjoying a butured and cut up tapir animal given to the fish by the local tribal indians who seem to idol and worship them for their ritual and tribal spiritual purposes. As we see the piranhas are still looking for a new fresh kill to put their teeth and gorging themselves upon when obtaining their next meal.

And then being very nice as a server, he then said to her thank you for showing me these monitor screens and then giving her another five pound note and then she smiled at him and didn't mention it anymore, and then she turned around and walked away looking at her walk away, dreaming.

A PATRON OF MONEY SAINTS

WHILE TWO MINUTES later in comes looking through the bar entrance is Harold Greenwald, a rich English financier of exotic expedition adventure looking at the seated Mr. Weiss drinking his beer and walks up to him and introduces himself to Mr. Weiss. Hello sir I am Mr. Greenwald and we have an appointment, yes Mr. Weiss agreed back to Mr. Weiss and Mr. Greenwald now both standing up then seated down in their leather chairs, (jennifer/waitress) came to them and asked Mr. Greenwald if he would like some refreshments, in which Mr. Greenwald said yes, I will have a Pilsner 12-once cold beer please, and then she left and two minutes later, she came back with the cold beer.

Mr. Greenwald said to Mr. Weiss, I have here in my hand that he took from his briefcase five-million american dollar cashier check for your south american expedition to western Brazil's mountainous region bordering Peru. Mr. Weiss, looking and listening while sipping his beer said to him thank you. Mr greenwald and then said the Barkly bank that will process your cashier's check is in miami, florida USA, once you arrive there you will go see a branch manager, Mr. Charles Evers, who will make all the necessary arrangements for your final trip to Brazil and will also provide with a armored river houseboat that you will name, and all the equipment you will use once you reach your destination, and gave him the check which he put into his attached case. Then Mr. Greenwald finished and paid for his beer, got up and said to Mr. Weiss By the way the bank manager has a daughter by the name of Paula Evers who will be joining your expedition tour, she happens to be a marine scientist who you might need in the Amazon rainforest, Mr. Weiss said back to him she is always welcome to join me and thank you for telling me and Mr. Greenwald said good luck on your sojourn to South America and then left the bar, and then five minutes later...

Mr. Weiss, drinking his ale beer, looked at the giant screen about trout fishing and then took out his coat pocket from the conference symposium event of late november brochure. Then the waitress came along and said is there anything else you would like and Mr. Weiss said another beer please if you may and she said thank you and two minutes later she came back with another Newcastle beer. Then glancing again at the two large monitor screens, looking a little to the right side of the bar he sees Mr. Terrance Smyth and Mr. Clive Bangor, who is also attending the conference here in London.

THEY COME IN PEACE, BUT LEAVE NOT SO NICE

MR. WEISS GETS up from his leather chair and joins Mr. Terrance Smyth and Mr. Clive Bangor who is kind of tipsy talking out loud, and perhaps drinking too much McDoodles Twenty-one old Irish Scotch whisky, in talking somewhat about Angkor Wat, and a secret find they are about to make when they are headed there next week. Mr. Weiss standing and listening to all of this, when now coming in the bar is wildlife naturalist photographer Nicole Hanes joining in the conversation and ordering another Mc Doodles whisky. Saying hello to us and then joining Hugo Hartford who also came in the bar, on the opposite side of the bar, and then she went to him there.

Mr. Weiss then went to the other side of the bar to join Hugo and Nicole and telling them their presentation was a good speech graphs about ancient civilizations before the incas arrival fifteen thousand years before, Then Hugo said thank you to Mr. Weiss and then Mr. Weiss said to Nicole

you're expose about natural wildlife genocide and depletion was most pro-
found, and she thanked me for recognizing that we must not be to so eager
to destroy our precious wildlife here on Earth. Then Mr. Weiss left the
two alone, waking back to the other side to Terrance and Clive and then
looking back at Nicole and Hugo, saw Hugo kissing her on the mouth and
getting very close and personal to each other in a lovers' romance embrace
and now coming into the bar…

A PROFESSIONAL TOUCH AND REFLECTIONS

DR. NEVILLE PENNYWORTH and his assistant Mr. Wesley Ross Pickford passing by me and speaking to me briefly about finding a pyramid half completed in southern Egypt under tons of sand and a tomb that has not been looted or ravaged by tomb raiders and pharoah robbers. The half completed pyramid under the sand is believed to be over thirty-five hundred years old, and structural engineers predicted it would have stood over 600-feet high. And when finished with there talk to me they then said join us, they then sit down in those comfortable leather wicker chairs and rotating fan blades, and acted very excited that within a few short days they will be going to this archeological site and will photograph the discovery find to the world via the world-wide internet in southern Egypt close to the nile river and twenty-five miles from the Sudan border. While sitting on the leather cushion chairs near the bar with his freshly ordered Newcastle beer, from (Jennifer/waitress) when a news flash on (TV) Tube from Brazil's western region came on, saying to the viewers that several people in western Brazil near the Peru border and also an area near the

Amazon river basin were savagely killed by an unknown large predator like creature. This makes seven deaths this year, already so near the cradle of the Andes mountain. With another seven inch incisor tooth, discovered on the scene and making it five tooths this year and it's only late november, with police Detective Torres, explaining that our crocodiles and anacondas here can exceed twenty feet in length and be quite toothy and can even easily crush and devour any human native or farmer or animal in its way as food prey, and not to worry for our police and security forces will now patrol the inland Amazon water tributaries way and side arteries with their high powered airboats for any sign of this large crocodile or anaconda and in its unwarranted killings here in the Amazon river basin.

AT THE HOTEL SYMPOSIUM

AS HE WAS finishing watching the (TV) tube, then suddenly a stranger comes and sits in front of him on the other side of the table and introduces himself as Billionaire Harold Ackerson, CEO and President of Wilkerson and Technology Industries LTD, perhaps you know of me, since I am at several times of the year, always in the news either good or bad.

As a billionaire and naturalist getting to the point with you Mr. Weiss, I am only one of the five largest contributors and supporters in preserving our past in museums or in books. And, I am grateful to you for addressing this issue at the conference, Mr. Weiss. We both wanted to know more about who we are and where we come from. Our billionaires are always giving away five hundred million dollars a year to the top ten worldwide museums, universities, forums and symposiums like this one today to better understand our human heritage. Jonathan Weiss, sipping his 22-ounce Newcastle beer, and snacking on pretzels said yes I know who you are, and you are a major benefactor here today attending this symposium at the center today to get some result you could be happy with. Mr. Clive Ackerson said to Mr. Weiss, you are quite astute and correct and why I am here now, and I really do care in my heart for our worldwide preservation of our humanity and to stop today our ignorance about our past in not correcting the mistakes we are now making, and what we are doing here today. At this conference we must provide for a change, and in moving forward in preventing our man made wars. And natural disasters from destroying our history's cultural past.

CAN A CHECK BOOK HELP

MR WEISS, WHAT I am now most interested in is you, and if you would be so grateful to me, and please listen to me now if you would go to South America for me, on a special assignment and taking out his checkbook and signing a check for two hundred and fifty thousand American dollars printed on its payable in any form. Jonathan Weiss looking briefly at the printed and signed check, said I am not one of your employees to fetch you a cup of coffee every time you need a cup refill, sir.

Mr, Ackerson said no, no coffee this time, and you totally miss understand me, what I want from you is to collect a particular certain dialect spoken that exist only at the cradle of the Andes mountain in brazil and Peru and today for it is called "Houaxueta", and only a small handful of their locals speak this dialect tongue, and what I must know from them and your translation is where is this cave that leads to a type of cave that leads to a strange world, a doorway if you please. Mr. Ackerson leaned over quietly to Mr. Weiss and saying quietly where is your bank in Chicago, and Mr. Weiss first thought briefly and then replying back to him and said to him, The United Trust Bank of Illinois to Mr. Ackerson, who said to Mr. Weiss, what I am about to show you is a very old book one hundred and fifty years old describing a kind of people that existed thirteen thousand years ago. In this book it has a language and symbols strange to mankind and unknown now or at that time thirteen thousand years ago. Two years ago I visited, "Piqua-Tu ruins 26 miles due east of Machu Picchu at the Pisac ruins when I met a classroom couple. Looking at the sights for their classroom report of ancient Aztec culture being escorted by this unknown young tour guide by the name of Emmanuel Ramon from Brazil who comes occasionally to Peru for work and when the couple left to too look around I went to this young tour guide and he spoke to me and said do you want to see something incredible and Mr. Ackerson said yes and please follow me up these steps to the back of this ruin about two hundred feet underneath some shrubs and twigs and Mr. Ackerson followed Ramon and what Ramon showed him was eleven blocks of granite that are well over thirteen thousand years old with t0hese strange markings on them, Mr. Ackerson. Looking at these markings to pictures of them and he said to Ramon what is that, and he that is the mountain plateau Auyan-tepul, where they came from not today but thousands of years-old Mr. Ackerson and he then thanked Ramon and they both joined the touring groups in front of the old Aztec ruins.

in Peru, And now speaking to Mr. Weiss drinking is ale beer, while I was there looking around I saw on some block stones was a strange symbols dialect on some stone block tiles showing a vertical cave going down this mountain plateau, I took some pictures, then I left and went down the small road bordering cliffs in my rented jeep thinking to myself what I just encountered. Driving down this steep mountainous roadway I came across a small village and a lone cafe and I went in to get a cold Coca-Cola bottle to drink and I was going back to by jeep when an old woman comes up to me speaking strange dialect of spanish with a little english thrown in looking hungry begging me for some food well then as a good deed I gave her twenty american dollars and instead of thanking me and leaving she gave me this old book and sad it is from the ancient gods I then said to her that is okay, do not worry but she was insistent that I have this ancient book, well i relented and excepted the book and I put it into my luggage bag in my jeep waving back to her and then I went back to her and gave the old woman, one hundred dollars and hen I left the small village and went to the main road to Lima Peru and then I headed back to England.

AN ANCIENT BOOK

IF YOU GO down to South America, If you want you can use copies of pictures and pages of the book that I have selected and down there you can use the book to help you navigate your surroundings and don't forget you are also looking for huge crocodile and anaconda snakes. And, then Mr Weiss bluntly said back to Mr. Ackerson, that I want ten million american dollars and some kind of armed and modified houseboat, trucks and jeeps to travel in and around the jungle forest and repelling equipment for cave exploration. Do we have a deal Mr. Ackerson, said yes we do Mr. Weiss and here are these copies and maps I am giving you and tomorrow you will contact my bank and hopefully you may be down there in two months and ackerson daid that I have to leave and here is my private business card and keep it for you may need it in the future, but before I leave waving to the waitress to come over here, he said to her, what is your biggest shrimp cocktail, Jennifer said back to him six American Gulf colossal shrimp, and then he said to her can you bring one order here with a 22-ounce Newcastle beer to my friend, Mr. Weiss. If you don't mind and she said back to him, it will be here in a jiff and before she leaves, he takes out fifty british pounds, I am paying this bill and given her the money and said to her keep the change, and she thanked him and walks away getting the order and then Mr. Ackerson left the bar.

INTO THE DREADED DARK RIVER HOUSEBOAT NEXT TO BEACH

TWO MONTHS LATER, now on board the "what's Next" houseboat, and then trotting along comes one local porter and guid, a quite knowledgeable fellow called Emmanuelle Ramon and bio-scientist, Paula Edwards. With Ramon and Paula standing by Mr. Weiss, and then Mr Weiss looking down on the turbid dark waters and sees 60 piranhas with Paula saying why so many staying so near the houseboat waters, and Ramon speaking to her says that houseboats are a great source for there food garbage we humans throw into the Amazon river and its easier for them to get their food from this way, then hunting and killing something coming along in the river in waiting for their food to come on by, Then Mr. Weiss saying to Ramon you certainly know your way around these parts, and Ramon saying back to Paula and Mr. Weiss, I do sir for I know these parts down here very well and Mr. Weiss said to him do you speak "Houaxueta", and Ramon said yes back to him and Mr. Weiss and Paula are now happy and Mr. Weiss said are there any flat top mountains near here and Ramon said yes, it is 60-miles away, kind of a flat 300 feet from its base is due west of here, if you follow this river we will reach the mountain base shore in the morning.

Paula said to Ramon are there any dangers ahead on this river and he said yes, many. Then Ramon said it is 5:30pm and I am getting some rest, and he then left them, on top of the second deck railing, Mr. Weiss said to Paula that Ramon is the best guide and hunter down here, Paula said to Mr. Weiss I am going down to get some sleep also, good night sir, and good night Paula, now standing by the railing he sipped his last drink 'Jack Daniels Bourbon', from his flask and smiling and saying to himself that Ramon knows about the plateau mountain, very good indeed. For I am a naturalist archeologist, Jonathan Weiss of the Field museum of natural history of Chicago, Illinois and is associate director and curator for the South American and Amazon Antiquities and extinct wildlife exhibit division.

For now today, I am after in my quest hunting down this serpent creature of death, today I am now day dreaming about my new fame worth more than $250,000 american dollars that will come soon with my picture on its front cover of all the magazines, and drinking a little of the daniels he suddenly by mistake, dropping and the two important pages he had in his pocket showing the the directions to the cave and the map of the river he must journey on, seeing the two papers going down into the piranha infested dark waters.

ALL SPEED FAST THERE IS DANGER AHEAD

THE NEXT EARLY morning with sebastian at the helm, Ramon comes up to the helm with two cups of coffee, with one for Sabastian thanking him, and while drinking the coffee looking looking out from the enclosed helm at the river they see a fork in the river one going to the left the other going to the right, Sebastian asked Ramon which way and Ramon said go to the right, if you take the left forked river ten miles ahead that way you will come to a very dangerous waterfall 100 feet high to its rocky bottom death by going left on that course, they took the right forked river preseeding now towards the brazilian plateau mountain, tepul, later that morning.

The Captain, Edmond Sanchez rang the houseboat warning bell 'danger ahead', Mr. Weiss, Paula and Ramon all came up to the wheelhouse from the mess quarters to see the slow cascading river coming to them, while the Captain taped his throttle full speed ahead and brace yourself it's going to be a rocky ride, then the captain increased his speed to a maximum of 10-knots and slowly but surely rode the houseboat up the on going rapids to the next river terrace landing escaping this immense danger upon them. And then after fifteen minutes the raids subsided and he slowed his throttle to four knotts going now further upstream to the mountain landing and shore about eight miles ahead.

One hour later after their breakfast standing by the railing Paula spoke to Ramon and said where are the piranhas, and Ramon said back to her that is strange, where are they? Mr. Weiss thought to himself and where are the crocodiles and anacondas? Paula said there is the mountain and Ramon, and Mr. Weiss said great our little adventure will now begin. Finally reaching the embankment shore at the stepping mountainous region known as the cradle of the Andes mountains base of the mountains, and the captain said I will land there next to the base shore and you can disembark into the jungle from there. The captain said I will stay here with one of my crewmen, Sebastian and my other two crewmen will accompany you Mr. Weiss, Paula and Ramon into the dense jungle.

ENTERING A ANCIENTS WORLD

THE JUNGLE WITH VINES

THE TRAVELERS GROUP (Mr. Weiss, Paula, and Ramon and two porters) enter the jungle with Paula noticing there are no birds making sounds and Ramon said maybe that a creature of some kind feeds upon them, with Mr. Weiss knows why? The travelers trekked 4 to 5 miles an hour, in thick brush with snakes and menacing small jungle cats looking at them and with large crawling insects nibbling at their exposed arms and face, with a grueling trek in hot, humid and eeking of almost blood sweat running down their faces, with those dam flies wanting to takLe your blood away, and after five hours they reached their goal they found a small stepping stone almost for professional wall climbers on the outside of the mountain from its base that appeared next to the jungle vines with those snakes and insects that may lead them to the top of the plateau and then they climbed hoping no dangers lie ahead. They climbed the cliff-edged stone terraces for over one hour and finally they reached the top plateau. Looking down three hundred feet into the Amazon jungle and further a field into the Amazon jungle river and their houseboat five miles away with their binoculars. They decided to stay the night because it is approaching 4:15 in the afternoon when they have to make base camp. They realized they had to start early the next morning.

A NIGHT OF HISSING TERROR AND GROWLS, AWAITS

THE A CAMP fire roaring and their food cooking and a fresh round of flask alcohol drinking, they talked about themselves while enjoying their meal with the five of them, totally falling asleep then they decided to go to sleep, at about 1:00 am the next morning they woke up to a growling sound coming from deep inside the vertical cave in the center of the plateau. The sound emitting was ebbing soft and loud lasting only about a half-hour duration time, and then silence. Mr. Weiss speaking to the group said this is a mythical creature that is alive today somehow. Ramon called this creature the terraboa. And, Paula said how did it come down there, and one of the porters said it was brought here from up there pointing to the sky? Mr. Weiss said that is impossible. It must be an offshoot from an anaconda water snake with Paula concurring with what Mr. Weiss said to them. Ramon said the people down here in the Amazon said these ancient beings from space came here thousands of years ago with Rapheal and Samuel saying yes. The next morning after a short breakfast the team of

Mr. Weiss, Paula, and Ramon and Rapheal, and one of the porters coming with Samuel staying top side as guard. Geared up in their mountain climbing and spinnaker equipment, "motorized backpack with oxygen, helmet light with side high beam flashlight, small digging tools, and empty satchel carry bag", and specialized rope to attach to the backpack and the rim of the vertical cave that is fifty feet wide is now all in preseeding to go down the vertical cave and to encounter the terrauna serpent of death.

A MIRACULOUS FIND UPON DEATH

GOING DOWN THE vertical cave, Paula said how smooth the cave walls are and Ramon said these are not natural cave vents, Paula. Mr. Weiss told Rlopapheal when landing on the ground we will set up a small temporary base camp, and Raheal said yes back. Now landing on the cave ground floor. They took their equipment off and together they started to explore the cave, after fifteen minutes they discovered something strange and interesting a very smooth wall and then repelling down and once on the cave floor we came to this great doorway leading into time and space, Mr. Weiss said while taking pictures of its writings and pictorial symbols like that from Egypt. Then after 15-minutes Paula heard in the background in one of the tunnel cave corridors a growling sound and Paula speaking to Pamon who is taking pictures and looking intensely on one of the wall door symbols and saying to Mr. Weiss, we can enter this doorway like a time machine, but how? And, Ramon looking around saw on the cave wall symbols like alpha like numerals. And as he touched one on the door and wall bezel numbers lighted up. But then he realized along with Mr. Weiss and Rapheal the sound nearby becoming louder in one of the corridors, and then they ran to their motorized harness equipment and put it on and said to Paul, Ramon and Rapheal go up now and they put on the harness backpacks and lifted them up with a top speed of 10-feet per second. Mr. Weiss staying behind and waiting, then in one of the corridors coming out into cave is a monster serpent that must be at least twenty feet in length that looks similar to a glorified frog and a lizard with a bio-luminescent skin and threatening reddish eyes, coming to him and then at the last second he takes several pictures of the creature, then presses his lift button and of he goes lifting off the cave floor at ten feet per second he then proceeds up the vertical cave tunnel to the surface and plateau with the others waiting for him.

OFF TO SEE A TERROR REPTILE, THE TERRAUNA SERPENT OF DEATH

IN LIMA, PERU at the El Diablo Hotel in room 27, Mr. ackerson is meeting with Hugo Hartford and Nicole Hanes about a deal to explore a cave with a secret entrance to a strange world of exotic animals from the past, if you would go down into this cave find this door like entrance and explore this strange world briefly I will give you a million dollars when you come back here to Lima, the bank here across the street has one million dollars in checking for you two, would you except this deal and mission with me, they left the room and in the hallway they talked about this offer and agreed and went back into room, and said yes to Mr. Ackerson and they all shaked hands. Mr Ackerson said to us you will meet at the wharf no. 15, pier seaplane with a gentleman by the name Michael Renner, an ex-green beret soldier that will escort you to the mountain plateau in the cradle of the Andes mountains.

juju

The next morning Mr. Ackerson escorted the couple to the wharf and a waiting seaplane and he introduced Me. Mr. Renner to them and then waiting at the pier to say goodbye as he watched the sea plane take off with Hugo, Nicole, and Mr. Renner flying to the cradle of the mountains and the mountain plateau.

The next morning after a restless sleep and after a brief and small breakfast, Mr. Weiss said to Ramon you will come down with me and Paula and Rapheal will stay here and if you see the monster go down the way we came up here, do you both understand and they agreed, yes. Mr. Weiss and ramon put on their equipment attached the ropes to the cave entrance rim, and after a few minutes went down three hundred to the floor of the cave and once down there they went to the small disk on the floor and Mr. Weiss took out the paper and gave it to Ramon who looked at it a few minutes and then entered the numeric code on the floor and then they got it right and the wall door began to open and inside the door there was nothing but six rims of aluminum like metal rims about ten feet wide and tall and that was it. Ramon looking at the paper got an idea then saw a second series of number like symbols, and then pressed each one and when completed the door began to close and then quickly Mr. Weiss ran to the inside of the doorway time machine, saying to Ramon to save me after a few minutes. Mr. Weiss standing in this doorway then was somehow tele-ported back thirteen thousand years ago. With incredible wildlife at that time. Then looking around he saw five alien reptilian beings coming up to him with ray guns aimed at him and then he was snatched and returned back to the cave with Ramon waiting outside with the opening up of a doorway time machine. Then getting together they heard loud growls and hissing sounds and quickly put on their equipment backpack harness and both Ramon and Mr. Weiss seeing the creature emitting electrical charges from its tongue coming close to them, pushed there harness lift button and up they went with a few seconds to spare before being electrocuted and eaten up by this strange alien creature to the surface plateau where they met Hugo, Nicole and Mr. Renner folding up parachutes with guns drawn meeting Mr. Weiss and Ramon. Mr. Renner is now tieing up Nicole, Sabastian and Rapheal, and Mr. Renner said if you make a simple move I am going to kill you. Then Nicole, Hugo Hartford along with Mr. Weiss and Roman suited up and are now at the rim and going down to the bottom floor of the cave Once down Mr. Renner with his automatic revolver aimed at Mr. Weiss and Ramon with Nicole and Hugo watching, started the time machine and the doorway began to open. Nicole went first then Hugo and Mr. Renner said to Mr. Weiss go ahead enter the machine and Mr. Weiss entered the machine and Mr. Renner ponting the revolver at Ramon goes ahead to start the time machine, as the doorway began to close, at the last second Mr. Weiss took the gun that was on Nicole loosely being held in her hand and took her revolver and quickly exited the wall door just as it closed shooting Mr. Renner two times in the left and right shoulders and then the wall doorway time machine closed and lighted up and Ramon entered the right two symbols on the time machine wall and in a few minutes they were sent 13 thousand years ago to a waiting fifteen reptilian soldiers somehow waiting for them, Hugo fired his revolver at them with their reptilian artificial body field emitter body protectors destroying the in coming bullets lobbed at them, and then they returned their shots with a specialized ray guns freezing them into suspended animation and then carrying them off to perform laboratory analysis on these hominids.

Back in the present in the cave Ramon took the revolvers from Mr. Renner and who is still alive and after a few minutes hearing the coming growls and hiss of the terranau serpent, the three of them saw the creature coming for them and then they quickly lifted off in their three back-pack harness to the plateau surface, once there they freed Paula, Sebastian, Raphael. And in the distance a helicopter was approaching them a the two-way radio Paula was carrying radio transmitter she opened up and he said this is Captain Edmond Sanches on the radio and said to Paula do you need help from us and she said yes we do, and he then said to her prepare us for landing on the mountain top and she said yes, and thank you.

A STEAMY SUMMER DAY IN AMAZONIA, 2019

BIRD AND CAT jungle It was a very hot at 113 degrees in late afternoon, after a torrential rain storm the night before at this base camp he nicknamed the 'ancients', when he was coming out of his tent yelling out loud and very mad carrying a artifact and ancient map, this was and enraged person, was the world famous 'from 'Egypt fame', British archeologist, Dr. Neville Pennyworth, in saying to his assistant Mr. Wesley Ross Pickford, and his chief guide Emmanuel Ramon, his chief person showing our way down here in the Amazon river jungle rainforest.

In this year of 2019, that he is speaking to the two gentlemen Mr. Pickford and Ramon, and he said to them, he went late in 2018 to a funeral and wake of Jonothan Weiss,(with Paula attending the funeral and to wish her respects to the deceased Mr. Weiss and talking briefly to Fran Weiss about her loss) the vice president and director of the field museum of natural history division of the South American antiquities and also folk legends museum in Chicago. Neville Pennyworth gave a private eulogy and sermon to him and then spoke to his wife, Fran Weiss. His now deceased widow and she said to me that I have been holding something he told me to give to you, from my deceased husband, Jonothan and here it is if you want to see what is inside it go ahead.

I said to her thank you but this belongs to you and not to me, I thank you anyway, so then she said back to me no, because the only person on this planet that he wanted to have this artifact, a giant nine inch tooth, a letter, two pictures, and a map, and this letter is especially for you and here it is for you, and if you like I will leave it on the table and leave you alone, she left and came back with tea and said it is your decision, only kind sir.

So, I pleased her and accepted them and took it home with me instead, and while home, I was sipping this blended scotch whiskey, while reading this letter, he wrote to me in his admiration and respect for me. And, a little envious of my accomplishments in the field of archeology and anthropology, and while continuing reading his letter he said in 2016 i went to the Amazon rainforest and with a help of a young emmanuel ramon I found this mountain plateau and the vertical cave on the brazil side with a secret to the ancients past.

I went to the Amazonian basin and went up the narrow trails leading up to a mountain sized 300 foot mountain plateau in the cradle of the andes mountain bordering peru and brazil and I found something so strange it appears to me as fiction on my part or anybody's part and what i'm telling telling you in what I found is this dreaded (curse) creature that is protecting or guarding this great door door like wall hiding something inside that is very alien and dangerous and it has been there for well over ten thousand years, old. The letter went on how to go there, and you must, if you can, hire a guide by the name of Emmmanuelle Ramon who will help you to enter the cave. Then the letter ended.

So gentlemen here we are now, I am, looking at mr. pickford and ramon. Knowing fully how I read these maps and what I want to find is a particular cavernous chamber of an alien artifact that may be true and not finding it on the map, I don't in my mind understand it. I am sure it was here, "said Ramon" ("thinking to himself that Mr. Weiss has been here three years ago and the creature is down there and I am afraid of it.

While neville is looking at this skull strange looking and odd cephalic large headed reptilian skulls that appear almost human to a certain degree, and I Presume them to be of some value when i take it back to London British Museum of Natural History and Ancient Artifacts and i have measured them to be at least over ten thousand years old here on this two hundred foot mountain with a shallow thirty foot small deep cave, and what I am looking for are not these skulls but a vertical cavern that will take us in looking for the Great wall door.

A STRANGE FATE AWAITS THEM AT THE MOUNTAIN PLATEAU AND ITS VERTICAL CAVE

Nevile Pennyworth said to everyone, What?

I WAS LOOKING for not these skulls but a vertical cavern that will take us to the Great wall door. These skulls are what I guess I did not come here for and are now unfortunately my consolation prize while looking at Mr. Pickford and Emmanuel Ramon in thanking them and can you please put these skulls into these large carrying plastic containers for my later studies at my pleasure in London in two weeks.

I thank you, said Dr. Pennyworth to Mr. Pickford and Emmanuel Ramon, again for coming down here with me in this hot and humid amazon jungle basin region to find this great wall doors that I must say appears to be fiction by Mr. Weiss or somehow it may have been here and is no longer and he said hoping that maybe it could be somewhere else, but where, but certainly this empty shallow vertical cave does not lead to the great wall door here.

As they are packing up to leave this mountain to go home. And then privately Rapheal said to Ramon that we need the work and our family depends on our work and money and Remon said it is very dangerous to go to that mountain plateau, raphael said maybe we can go and not involve ourselves to much in the dangers there, and Ramon said okay we will tell them. Five minutes later both Ramon and Rapheal said to Neville and Pennyworth we know where this mountain plateau you are looking for is, it lies thirty miles north from here, and we can take you there, and Neville and Wesley smiled, laughed and said thank you back and why did you not say to us earlier, because that mountain plateau is dangerous and you may not survive if you go down into the cave, for it contains a creature truly, dangerous. And, Pickford said we have revolvers, grenades, and automatic rifles we will survive. And later they went off in their one truck and one land rover jeep along a congested and dense jungle but passable with an ancient road way to the mountain plateau and the vertical cave.

THE MOUNTAIN PLATEAU OF THE COMING DEATH

THE APPROACHING THE mountain plateau of death, they saw a small helicopter flying overhead and headed for the plateau. Dr. Pennyworth and Ramon in the front landrover jeep and in the rear in the Mercedes truck carrying Mr. Pickford and Rapheal along with two porters in the back cabin. After twenty minutes they arrived at the base of the mountain in a clearing and they parked their vehicles and off loaded their mountain gear along with equipment they may need going down the vertical cave to the great door door after ten minutes they started climbing the mountain on the stone cliff steps side and it wasn't easy but they made it in one hour and five minutes and once they reached the top they met Director Mr. Harold Bangor of the London Museum of Antiquities and archeology a subdivision of the London Museum of natural History and with Miss Paula Evers of Miami Marine life aquarium who made base camp and started cooking food for the night stay and she said to them you are welcomed to join in and Mr. Pickford took out the Mc Doodles scotch whiskey and poured some with everybody enjoying sausages and beans, and whiskey.

Dr. Pennyworth asked what are we doing here I am a naturalist and I am anxious to see the wildlife thirteen thousand years ago, last year Iwent to Clive Ackerson and he gave me a copy of the ancient symbol writings of the notes he took down here so I went to Herald Bangor and it took him six months to figure out the symbol writings with the aid of a super AI computer and Harold wanted to come a long and I needed the Company and here we are with you and I believe we can team up and see what's inside the alien world past the door time machine, do we have an understanding and Dr. Pennyworth agreed along with Wesley Pickford and Ramon smiling at Paula Evers and her smiling back at Ramon. That night at 12:30 they were awaken by loud growls coming deep inside the vertical cave for about 15 minutes and then silence the creature is awake and looking for food at the same time on of the porters was taking a leak near the cliff and saw the creature in the jungle going to the river with Paula, Dr. Pennyworth, Mr. Pickford and Ramon looking on at the creature with its bio-lumense skin going to the river tributary for food and Paul said there is another way in the mountain cave then up here on the plateau, Pickford said we should go down now while the creature is gone and look at the great wall time machine door and they all agreed and Paula, Mr. Bangor, Mr. Pickford and Ramon suited up in their backpack motorized harness secured their line to the rim of the vertical cave and after a few minutes down they went over three hundred feet to the bottom ground flooring and entered the cave and the great wall like door. Ramon said I know how to start, open and engage the time and Paula said great and they (Paula, Mr. Bangor and Dr. Pennyworth) entered the time machine and Ramon engaged the to close symbol and is now starting the time machine closing the time and with Mr. Pickford on the small window inside the time machine then Ramon engaged the machine to send them 13 thousand years ago in time. Back in time they saw what life was like with many animals now extinct and walking about they saw their disbelief one very large landing flying saucer in the near distance with over 100 soldiers entrapping animals and putting them into holding cages, then the landed flying saucer with two of the lookout soldiers seeing them and waved to the other soldiers and are now coming to the interlopers and back in the cave Ramon said I have funny feeling and started the time machine and realizing what with the reptilian alien soldiers coming very near them on the other side, saw the pulsed whirling vortex energy field light up and Paula, Dr. Pennyworth and Mr. Bangor hurried up and jumped into the swirling pulsed energy emitter field and as the reptilians almost reached them they disappeared and now coming to the present Paula saw Ramon, and Pickford in the small window screen and now the time machine has stopped and the doorway opened up and they got out and went to the cave and in the distance of the cave corridors they heard a faint growling and hissing sound and quickly they put on their backpack motorized harness now with the growling sound coming very loud and they all see the creature come out of the corridor tunnel and into the main cave and all of them pressed their lift buttons on their harness and up they went leaving the creature down on the floor of the cave and after a couple of minutes they reached the rim of the top plateau cave surface and said to each other what the hell did we just saw down there, Mr. Bangor said this is a strange early life on Earth that is somehow colonized by these reptilian aliens but how and why are they not here today, this creature who tried to kill and may be eat us and to how is that down there to begin with and to explain with the plateau surface people realizing that down below is becoming dangerous in the vertical cave and its bottom surface.

And in the time machines being engaged and sent back 13, 000 years ago and a waiting reptilian aliens for there return back here in the time machine that is finally showing a whirling vortex lighted emitter field and then the aliens on their levitation hoverboards went into the whirling lighting emitter field and went off to thirteen thousand years into the future.

That night with all sleeping on the surface plateau except for Paula who with Ramon and Rapheal climbed down the mountain and once they reached the base jungle floor in trying to find the cave entrance somewhere near the base, and while in the amazon jungle up, coming from below are five reptilian soldiers coming to the surface and with their ray guns froze Dr. Pennyworth, Mr. Bangor, Wesley pickford, and the one sleeping porter and took them down the vertical cave and the aliens entered them in the time machine doorway and they went back to the past.

THE END OF TIME

WHILE THE REPTILIAN aliens were on the plateau top surface, the small group of Paula Evers, Ramon and Rapheal was searching and found the entrance to the cave and going in they heard a faint growl and hissing sound and moved on to the smaller tunnel corridors in trying to escape the creature and they found the the right tunnel leading them to the main cave near the doorway and they saw the reptilian aliens carry the four humans into the the doorway time machine and the one alien engaging the machine quickly and then went inside the time machine before it closes and is once engaged and then Ramon and Paula quickly went to the time machine that was about to send them back in time, and at the wall control panes paula said to Ramon enter this symbol and do not question it for it will work Ramon entered the symbol and then the machine started and began to send the reptilians back 13 thousand years ago except for the four humans, who stayed phased behind on the floor, and then Ramon entered this symbol blocking the return of the aliens back here, and on the wall of the time machine the four rravelers began to unfreeze and thaw out and meeting Paula and Ramon, and Rapheal at the door which is opening up and after a couple of minutes they were completely alert and when they began to hear the creature becoming louder Paula and Ramon said to them let us go now, they by pased the creature and went outside the cave and ran to their truck and landrover now followed by the creature with the interlopers reaching the truck they got out their armrmrnts and just in the nick of time, because the creature was only thirty feet from them emitting 1,400 volts of electric energy from its tongue at them and the interlopers opened up and fired and ponding the creature with elephant killing bullets from their AR-15 rifle and their automatic revolvers and it onyly made a small dent in the body of the creature quickly. Bangor gave each one of the interlopers grenades and said to them together take out the pin throw the grenades under the creature and they did and let go of the grenades all landed under the creature except for the one which went inside the mouth of the creature grabbing and eating it and then they all went for cover behind the truck and landrover and then the grenades exploded sending its body pieces all about and splashing its destroyed innards even on the interlopers and they got up together and congratulate each one for a job well done and in the morning at the mountain plateau top they all said no one must know of this place with everybody saying amen, and a little later down at the truck and landrover they all left plowing through the dense jungle and all of them going home alive.

THE END? AND, MAY IT COME SOON ENOUGH?

INSIDE THE CAVE at the doorway time machine and on the wall control panels there is one symbol lighting up that Paula and Ramon did know about the entire panel with that symbol now is engaged and the time machine is on and fully working and inside the doorway time machine comes two humanoid entities and then the time machine stops, and is opening up and out comes Nicole and Hugo half naked and in a complete zombie state walking out of the cave and into the Amazon jungle walking fifteen miles to the general outpost store on an old dirt Amazon road…?

The zombies, Hugo and Nicole, were walking and not even a jaguar cat who did not want to do anything with them. And after a few minutes walking they stopped and a jeep came by and it was from a construction road building working crew from fifteen miles away. Then then when the jeep stopped and the driver looked at the two half naked couples with their tattered clothes and zombie like behavior and then he went and contacted by radio call the construction company forman telling them what happened, and they said take them to the outpost general store, market and small cafe and, he carefully put them into the jeep and drove twelve mile down the dirt road to the store and also calling the police in the outpost store to send a medic helicopter to pick them up and send them to the Amazon general hospital one hundred miles away, with the police at outpost station 56 that is fifty-five miles away to pick them up also at the general store.

Two hours later at the general store cafe section the two zombie couples were being inspected by Captain Torres and his daughter Isabel Toress who is also the Emergency Medical Advisor for the police in the Amazon, and looking at them in both their eyes of Nicole and Hugo, and she found them all black with no signs of color or life in the two of them. Next she prodded them with a pin and nothing no reaction to the pain of the prick and then checked their heart pulse and it was very low less than fifty beats per minute and then Isabel and Captain Torres said to each other we have to go to the Amazon General Outpost Hospital and to ICU and have Dr. Harras look at them and in a few minutes they went off in there helicopter and one hundred and fifty eight miles southeast to the hospital there.

Once at the hospital at the ICU room Dr. Harras came in and inspected the two couples and their food intake with intravenous feeding. They started slowly to come alive and then two days later an X-ray was taken of Nicole and found out she was having a baby. With increasing contractions and labor pains were hitting Nicole very hard one of the Dr's and two of the nurses came in the ICU and said it's time we go into the operating room she is about to deliver a baby and in the operating room the baby of Nicole was delivered and every body there was a gasped and the nurses crying what they were looking at were a half human and a half reptilian baby with a small tail in its rear. Dr. Harras called Captain Torres to come to the hospital and he and Isabel came and saw the baby and Captain Torres contacted Neville Pennyworth to come down to western Brazil and to the hospital if you can kindly come and he agreed and he also contacted Paula, a specialist of fish and reptile studies.

A FUTURE TERROR COMING SO YOUNG

 Paula, Benjamin Stokes, Neville Pennyworth, Captain Torres, Isabel Torres and Dr. Aldor Bormann, The Neurologist, and the Dr. Harras, all looked at the new baby that is growing fast (it is already five days, one and a half human years old with twice the intelligence I.Q. of a full human, it has human like feet, almost monkey hands, a larger head than humans, with two incisor half inch teeth, and no hair but a reptilian soft skin), Dr. Harras said it, the baby can stay at the hospital in our converted stock room and we can monitor it there, for right now we do not know the sex of it but it will show up later as it grows. It was born with a envelope around it and we took it off two days later because that envelope kept him warm and secure, and now it is discomfort to it, and now begging to be playful and believe it or not it smiles a lot. Now coming into the room is Colonel Edwardo Harras brother to the doctor, and the colonel of the brazilian air force responsible for this entire Amazon area for five hundred square miles. May we all speak in the conference room about this baby that Nicole and Hugo who seem to be okay and fully alive and aware with full color in their eyes and eating very well. You see everybody my brother is continuously communicating with me. The reason I am here is The Brazilian Government believes there is an alien presence in this country and I do not mean the baby, I Would like to know how this is possible and, Dr. Neville Pennyworth and Paula also spoke to the Colonel and told him the entire story of what happened at the mountain plateau and in its cave with the alien wall doorway time machine portal.

One week past by in the morning at 9:30 am and Hugo and Nicole are doing just fine with the neurosurgeon doctor speaking to them said we removed a oblong small pill size device attached to your upper back neck to your brain do you know anything about what it does, they said no, and thanked the doctor for removing it and then a little later one of the nurses discovered that the baby was found dead with its lungs completely dead with no oxygen reaching its body. Dr. Harras was Immediately notified and told later to Hugo and Nicole and said after examination the two parts of the baby, one human the other reptilian mutation alien were not compatible with each other biological make up structure, somehow the human part was overpowering the alien part and a massive system break down occurred and it died sometime in the early morning. Hugo and Nicole for the scientific community it is a great loss, but for us we are grateful it is dead, you two seem to be fully alive and healthy the doctor said to them if you want you may leave and go back to England where I believe you have a home there and they said yes we have contacted the airport and they are sending an helicopter tomorrow morning to pick us up and, then the postal delivery this morning sent a check for one million american dollars to our hospital, it is from Nicole and Hugo and we thank you very much for the kind generous offer, the couple said to the doctor don't mention it for it belongs to you all for the kind work you do here for people here in the Amazon Jungle because you saved our lives we are very happy for that. And, also take care of the baby corpse and the doctor may fully diagnose its death and do a complete biological investigation and autopsy of its systems failure and the doctor said thank you. Meanwhile at the mountain plateau there is military activity with the colonel and his men are repelling down the vertical cave and reaching the bottom floor of the cave and after fifteen minutes found nothing, no great wall doorway and no wall control panel, absolutely nothing down here but one of the men found a seven inch tooth that appears to be very old, and the men later repelled up the vertical cave to the surface top and gave the colonel the tooth and said I will keep this as a souvenir and said to his men there seem to be now no alien invasion of Brazil or Earth and boarded the Brazilian air force helicopter and took off for the Brazilian capital to give a boring report to the top brass while flying in the helicopter that he learned from his brother that when the baby died, its body emitted a strange reptilian not human smell, and as he concluded the report flying in his helicopter to Brazilia, with this paper review he is holding, he has determined that this case is now closed speaking to his men on board, and seeing the military helicopter go into the far distance.

THE END: OF INTERLOPERS? OR IS IT?